# GUARDIANS OF THE GALAXY
## GALAXY'S MOST WANTED

ROCKET RACCOON

GROOT

WRITER **WILL CORONA PILGRIM**

ARTIST **ANDREA DI VITO**

COLORIST **LAURA VILLARI**

LETTERER **VC'S CLAYTON COWLES**

ASSISTANT EDITOR **MARK BASSO**

EDITOR **BILL ROSEMANN**

EDITOR IN CHIEF **AXEL ALONSO** CHIEF CREATIVE OFFICER **JOE QUESADA**
PUBLISHER **DAN BUCKLEY** EXECUTIVE PRODUCER **ALAN FINE**

MARVEL STUDIOS:
VP PRODUCTION & DEVELOPMENT **JONATHAN SCHWARTZ**
SVP PRODUCTION & DEVELOPMENT **JEREMY LATCHAM**
PRESIDENT **KEVIN FEIGE**

ABDO
Spotlight

**ABDOPUBLISHING.COM**

Reinforced library bound edition published in 2016 by Spotlight,
a division of ABDO, PO Box 398166, Minneapolis, Minnesota 55439.
Spotlight produces high-quality reinforced library bound editions for
schools and libraries. Published by agreement with Marvel Characters, Inc.

Printed in the United States of America, North Mankato, Minnesota.
042015
092015

THIS BOOK CONTAINS
RECYCLED MATERIALS

marvelkids.com
© 2015 MARVEL

**LIBRARY OF CONGRESS CATALOGING-IN-PUBLICATION DATA**

Pilgrim, Will Corona.
  Galaxy's most wanted / story by Will Corona Pilgrim ; artist, Andrea Di Vito ;
colorist, Laura Villari ; letterer, VC's Clayton Cowles.
     pages cm. -- (Guardians of the galaxy)
  "Marvel."
  ISBN 978-1-61479-391-5
1.  Graphic novels. [1. Graphic novels.]  I. Di Vito, Andrea, illustrator. II. Title.
  PZ7.7.P528Gal 2016
  741.5'973--dc23
                        2015005209

**Spotlight**

A Division of ABDO
abdopublishing.com

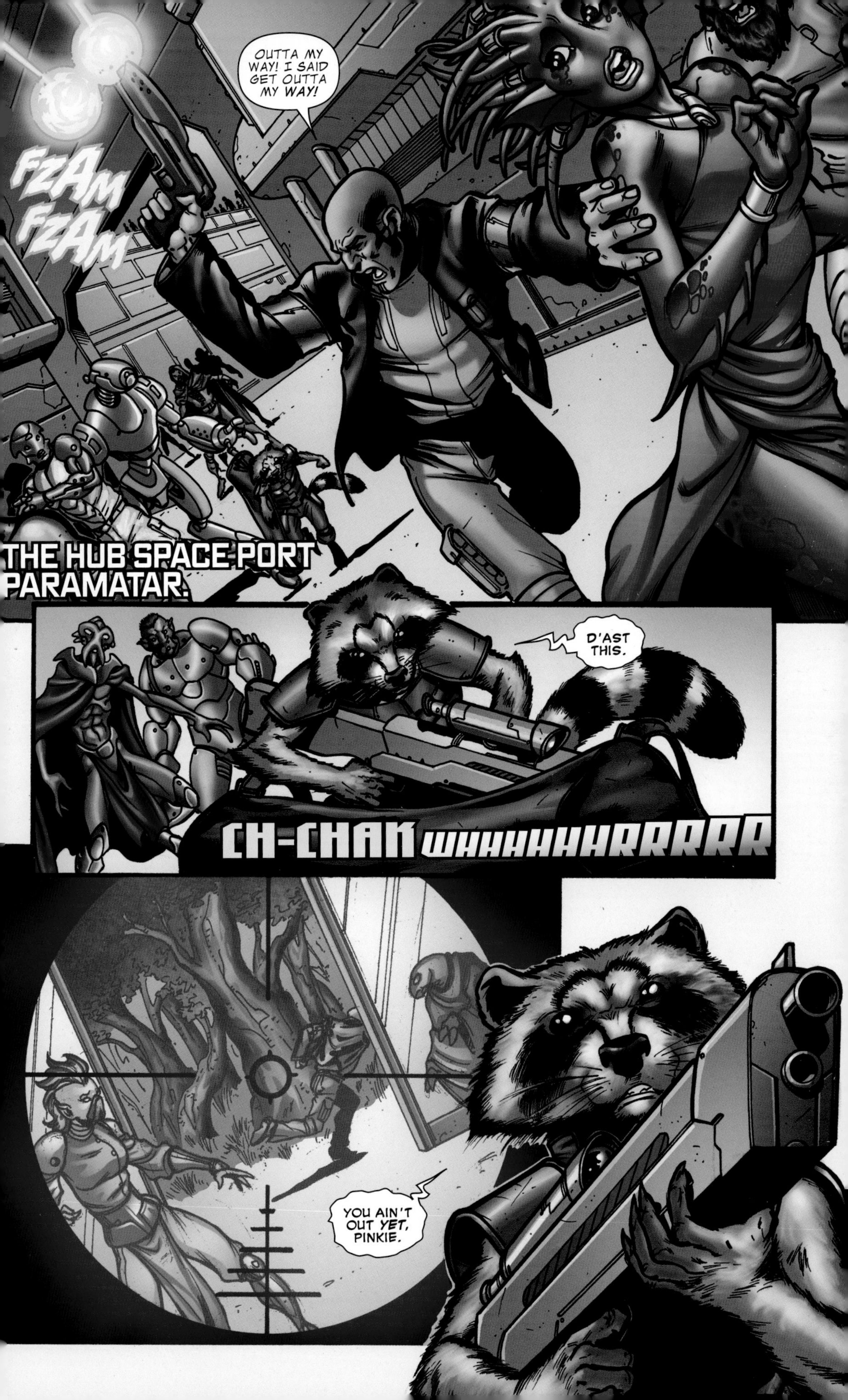
OUTTA MY WAY! I SAID GET OUTTA MY WAY!
FZAM FZAM
THE HUB SPACE PORT PARAMATAR.
D'AST THIS.
CH-CHAK WHHHHHHRRRRR
YOU AIN'T OUT YET, PINKIE.

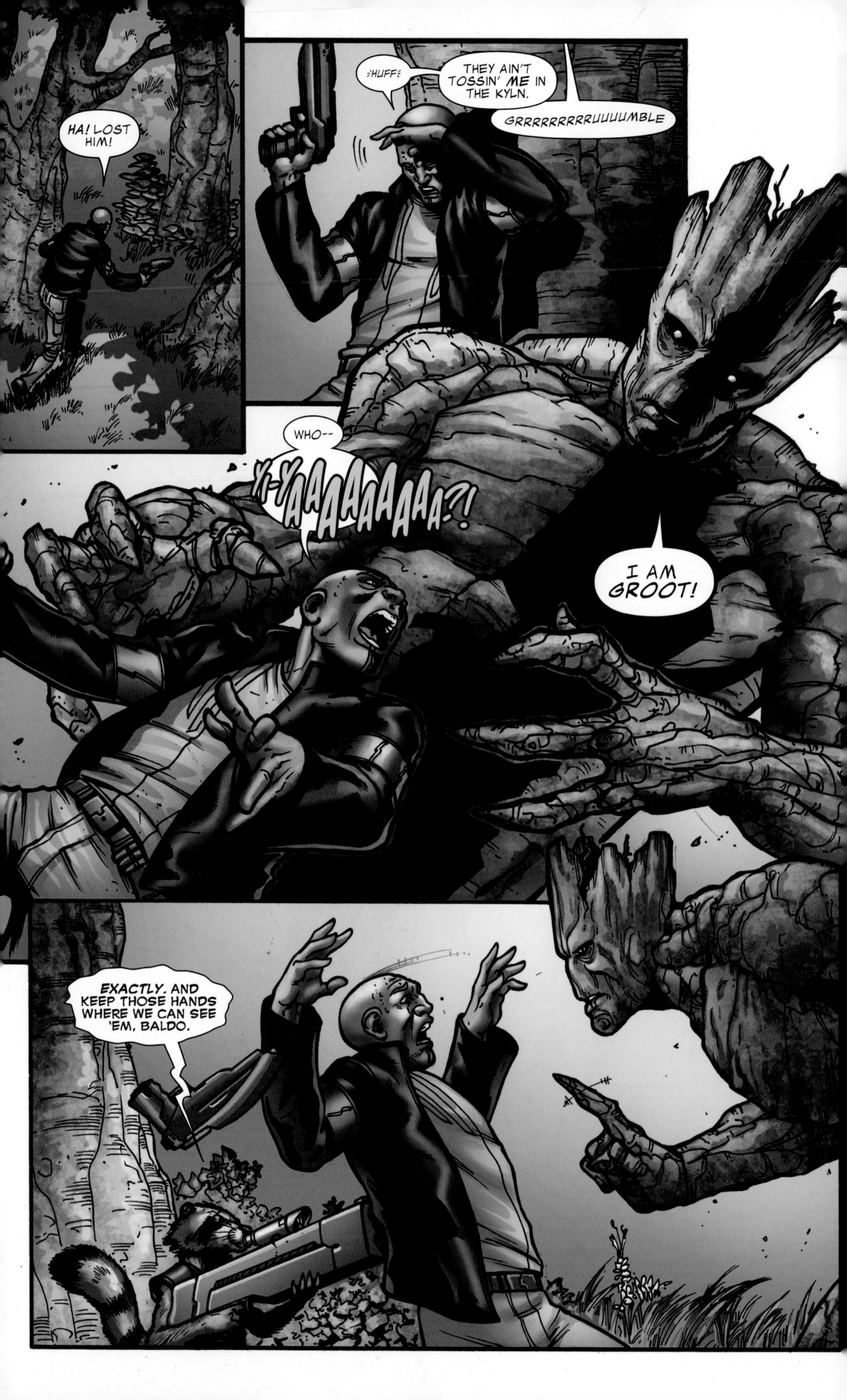
HA! LOST HIM!
HUFF
THEY AIN'T TOSSIN' ME IN THE KYLN.
GRRRRRRRRRUUUUMBLE
WHO--
YI-YAAAAAAAAA?!
I AM GROOT!
EXACTLY. AND KEEP THOSE HANDS WHERE WE CAN SEE 'EM, BALDO.

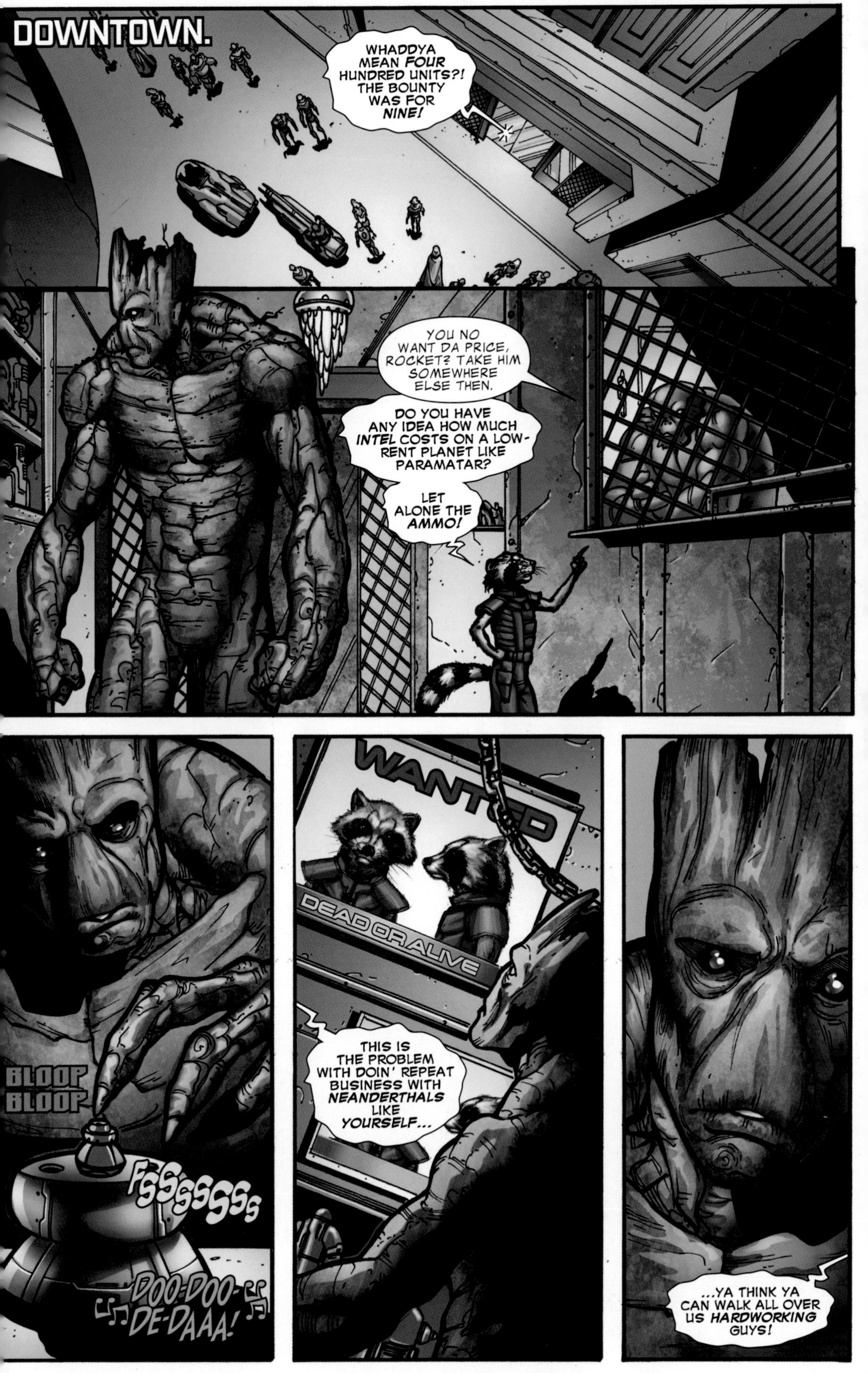
DOWNTOWN.
WHADDYA MEAN FOUR HUNDRED UNITS?! THE BOUNTY WAS FOR NINE!
YOU NO WANT DA PRICE, ROCKET? TAKE HIM SOMEWHERE ELSE THEN.
DO YOU HAVE ANY IDEA HOW MUCH INTEL COSTS ON A LOW-RENT PLANET LIKE PARAMATAR?
LET ALONE THE AMMO!
BLOOP BLOOP
FSSSSSSS
DOO-DOO-DE-DAAA!
WANTED
DEAD OR ALIVE
THIS IS THE PROBLEM WITH DOIN' REPEAT BUSINESS WITH NEANDERTHALS LIKE YOURSELF...
...YA THINK YA CAN WALK ALL OVER US HARDWORKING GUYS!

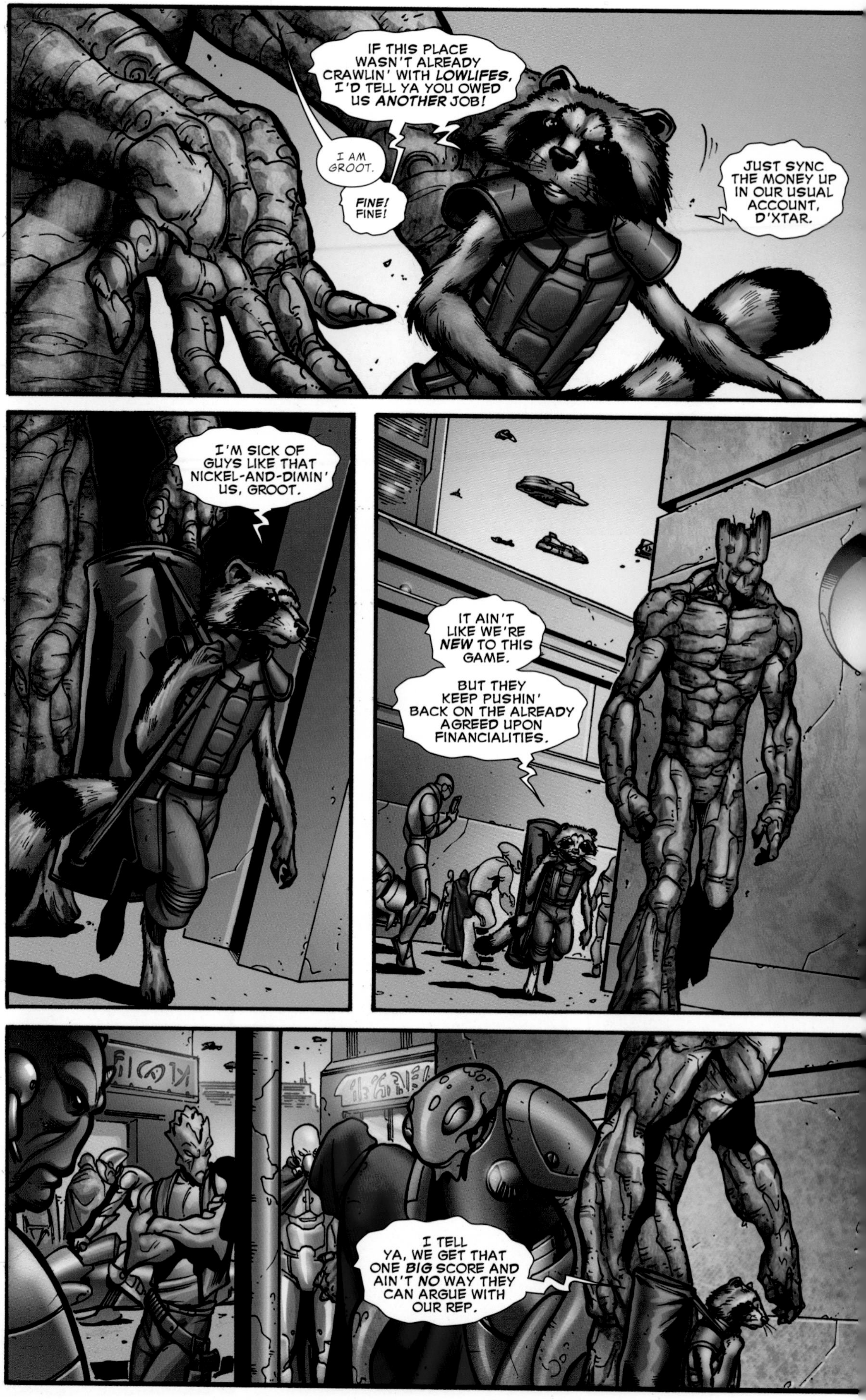
IF THIS PLACE WASN'T ALREADY CRAWLIN' WITH LOWLIFES, I'D TELL YA YOU OWED US ANOTHER JOB!
I AM GROOT.
FINE! FINE!
JUST SYNC THE MONEY UP IN OUR USUAL ACCOUNT, D'XTAR.
I'M SICK OF GUYS LIKE THAT NICKEL-AND-DIMIN' US, GROOT.
IT AIN'T LIKE WE'RE NEW TO THIS GAME.
BUT THEY KEEP PUSHIN' BACK ON THE ALREADY AGREED UPON FINANCIALITIES.
I TELL YA, WE GET THAT ONE BIG SCORE AND AIN'T NO WAY THEY CAN ARGUE WITH OUR REP.

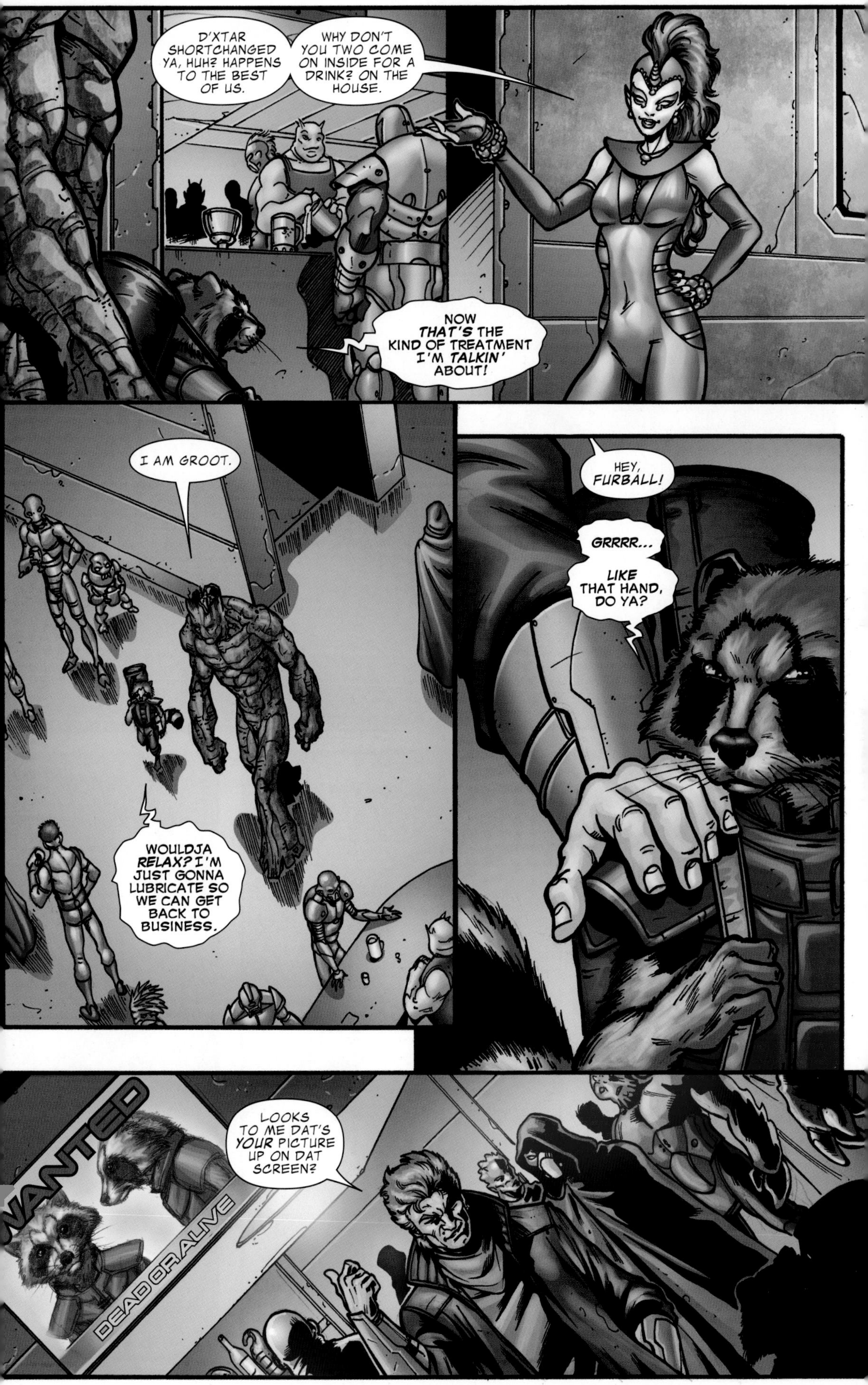
D'XTAR SHORTCHANGED YA, HUH? HAPPENS TO THE BEST OF US.
WHY DON'T YOU TWO COME ON INSIDE FOR A DRINK? ON THE HOUSE.
NOW THAT'S THE KIND OF TREATMENT I'M TALKIN' ABOUT!
I AM GROOT.
WOULDJA RELAX? I'M JUST GONNA LUBRICATE SO WE CAN GET BACK TO BUSINESS.
HEY, FURBALL!
GRRRR... LIKE THAT HAND, DO YA?
WANTED
DEAD OR ALIVE
LOOKS TO ME DAT'S YOUR PICTURE UP ON DAT SCREEN?

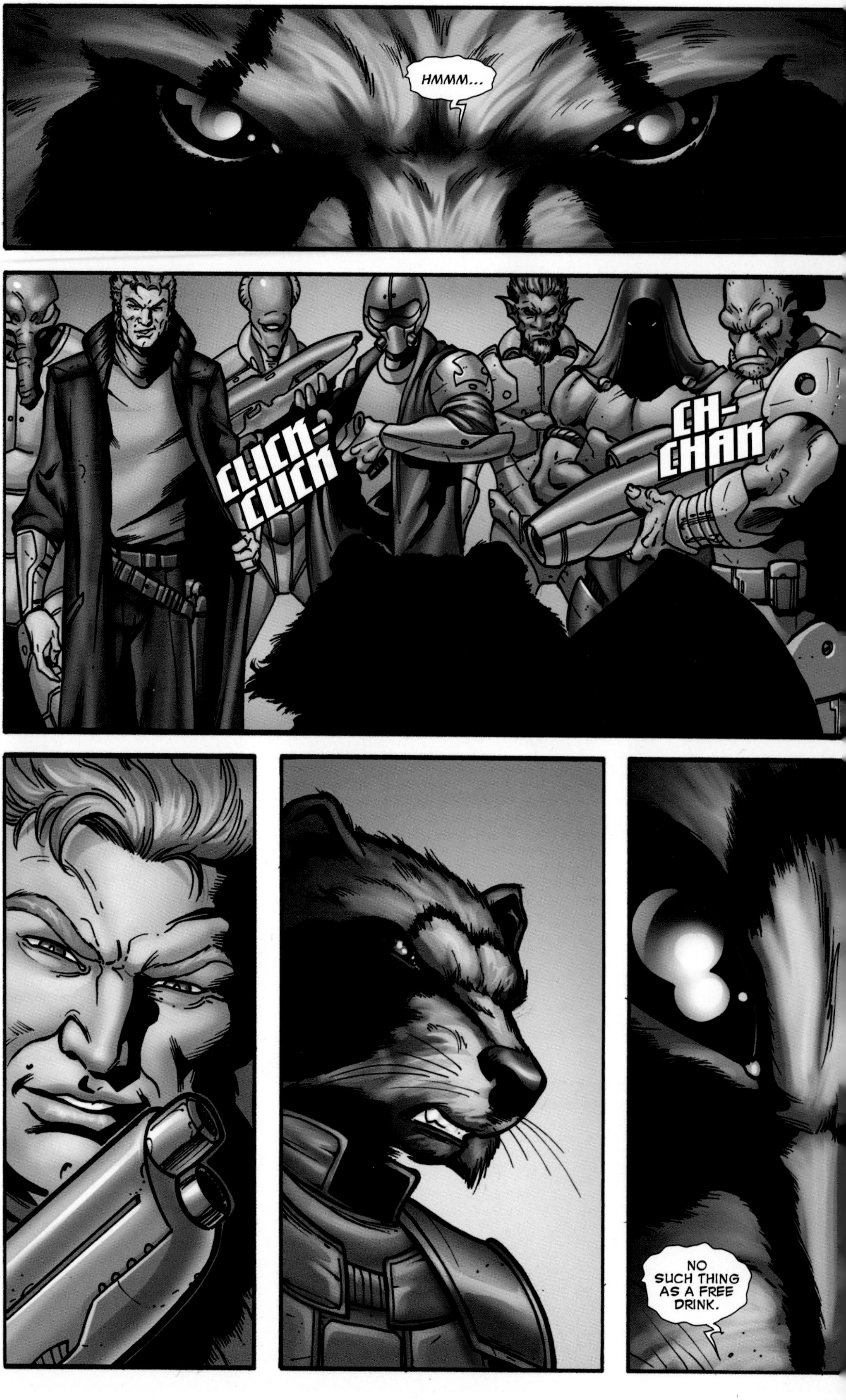
HMMM...
CLICK-CLICK
CH-CHAK
NO SUCH THING AS A FREE DRINK.

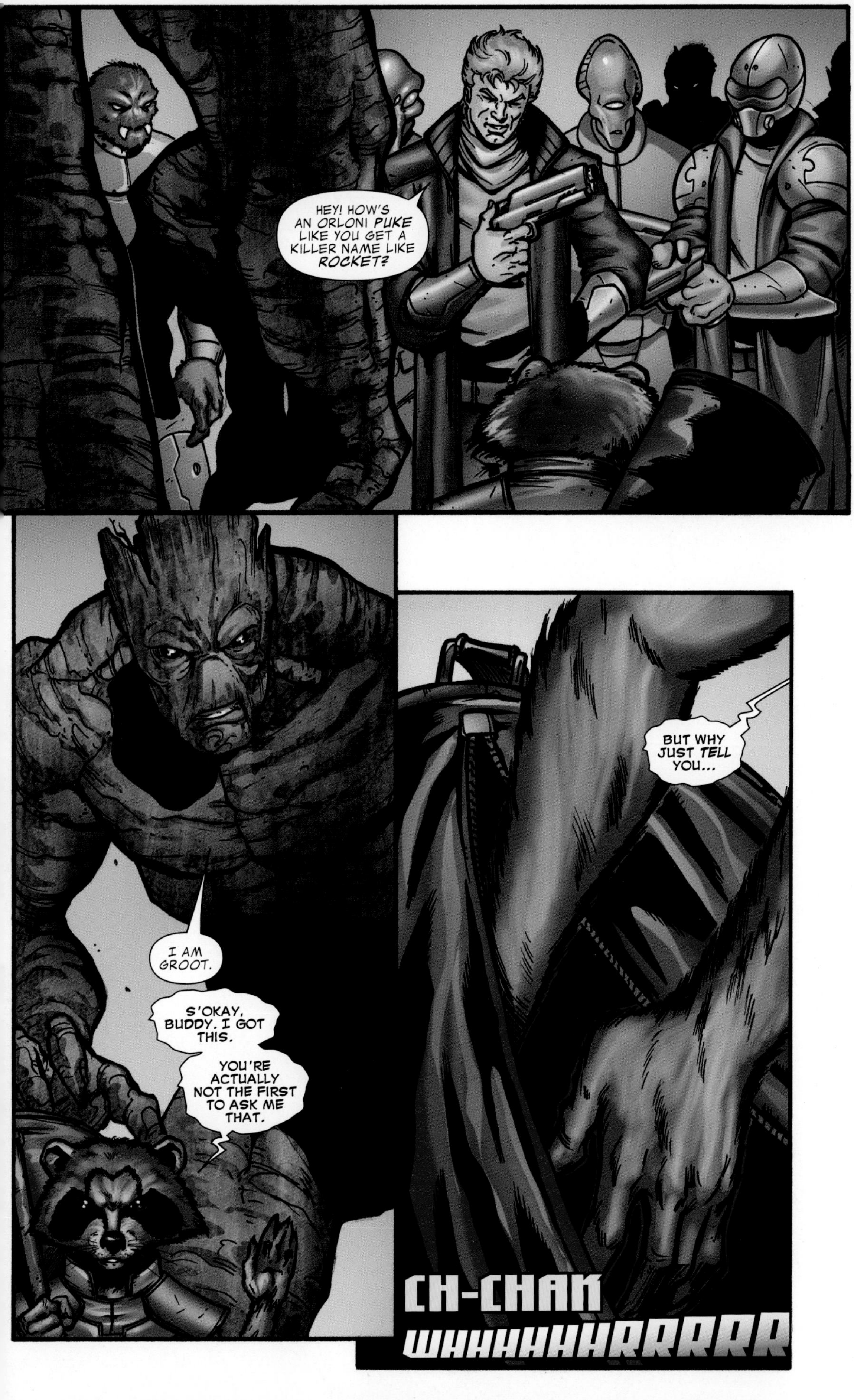
HEY! HOW'S AN ORLONI PUKE LIKE YOU GET A KILLER NAME LIKE ROCKET?
I AM GROOT.
S'OKAY, BUDDY. I GOT THIS.
YOU'RE ACTUALLY NOT THE FIRST TO ASK ME THAT.
BUT WHY JUST TELL YOU...
CH-CHAK
WHHHHHHRRRRR

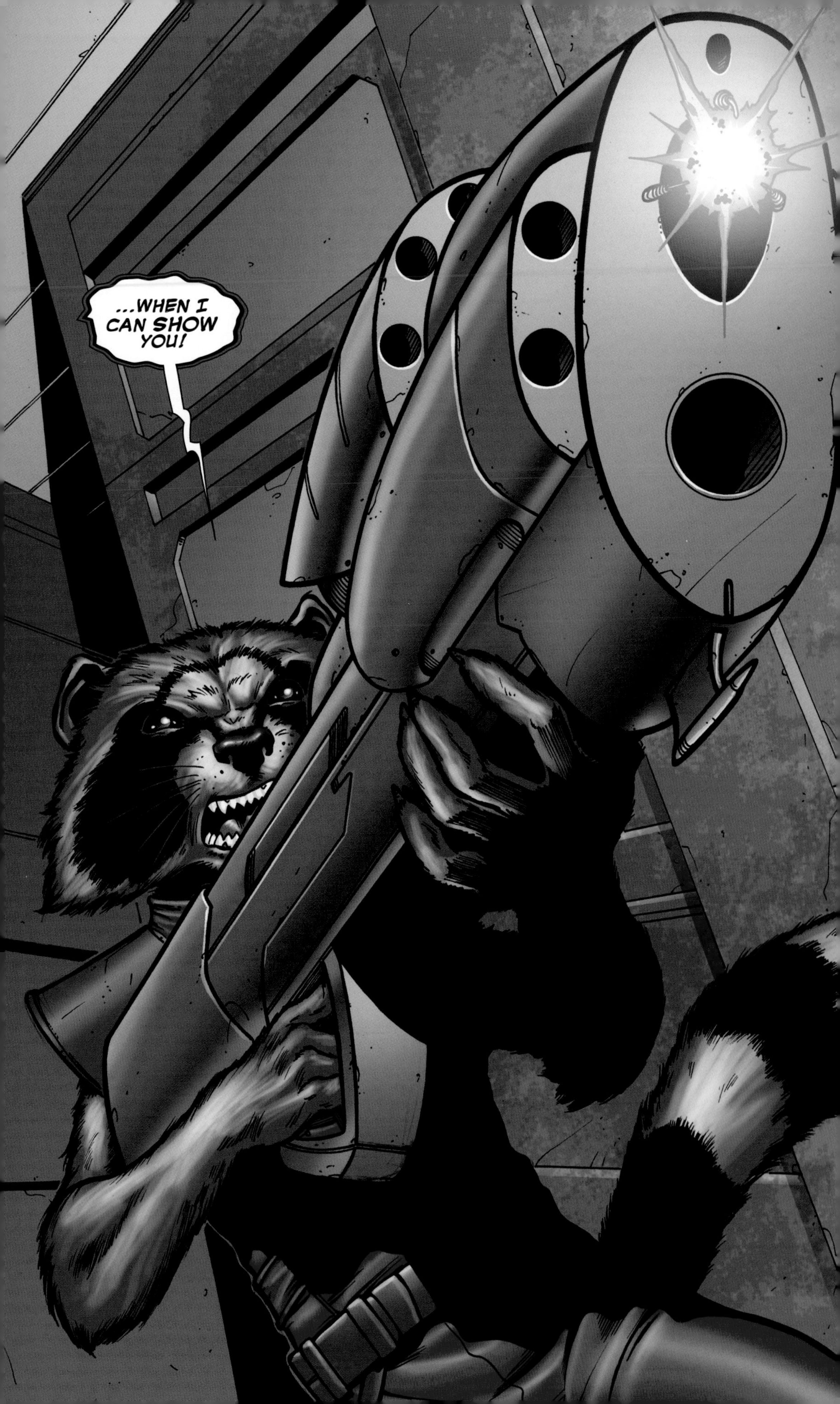
...WHEN I CAN SHOW YOU!

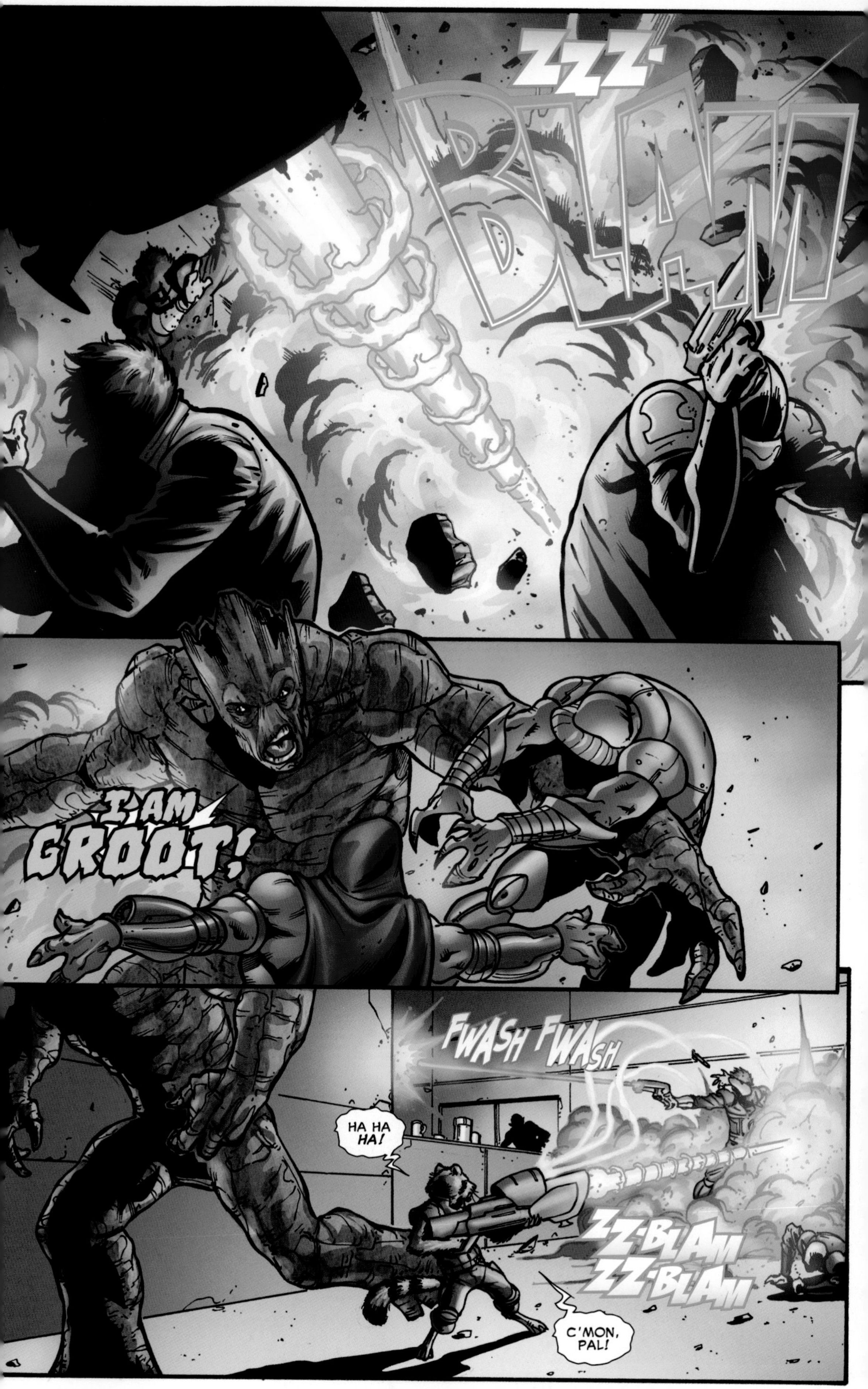
ZZZ-
BLAM
I AM GROOT!
FWASH FWASH
HA HA HA!
ZZ-BLAM ZZ-BLAM
C'MON, PAL!

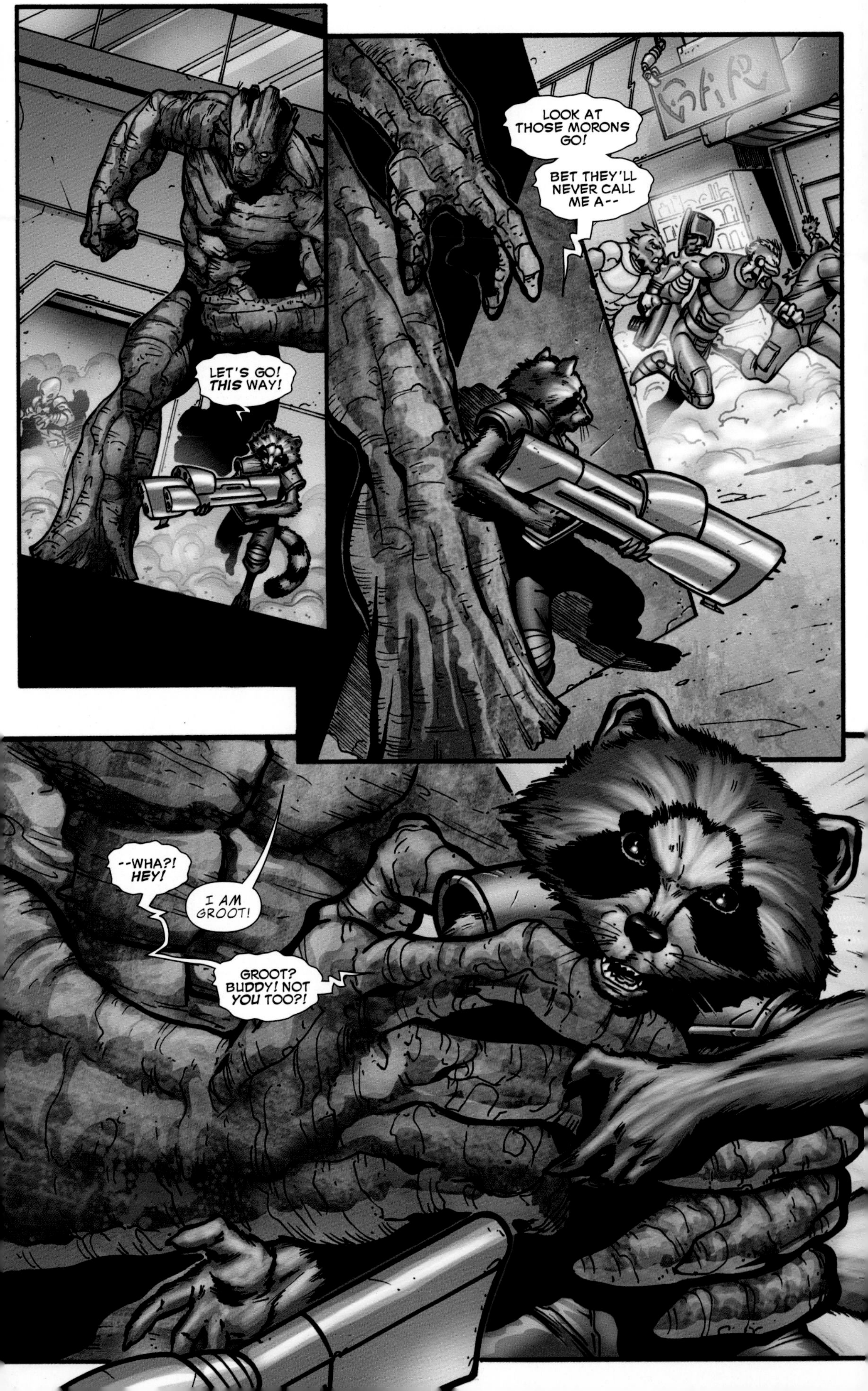
LET'S GO! THIS WAY!
LOOK AT THOSE MORONS GO!
BET THEY'LL NEVER CALL ME A--
--WHA?! HEY!
I AM GROOT!
GROOT? BUDDY! NOT YOU TOO?!

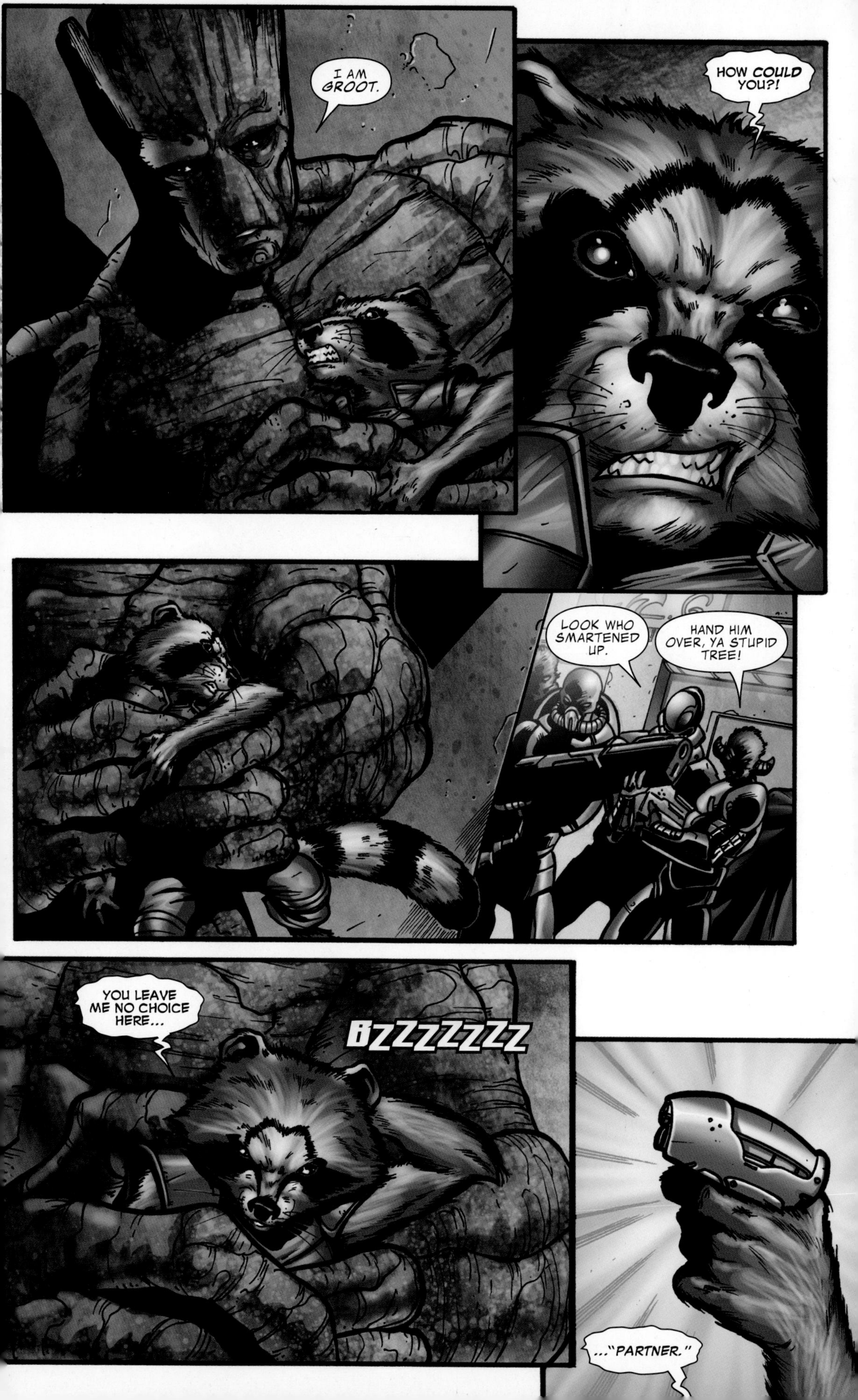
I AM GROOT.
HOW COULD YOU?!
LOOK WHO SMARTENED UP.
HAND HIM OVER, YA STUPID TREE!
YOU LEAVE ME NO CHOICE HERE...
BZZZZZZZ
..."PARTNER."

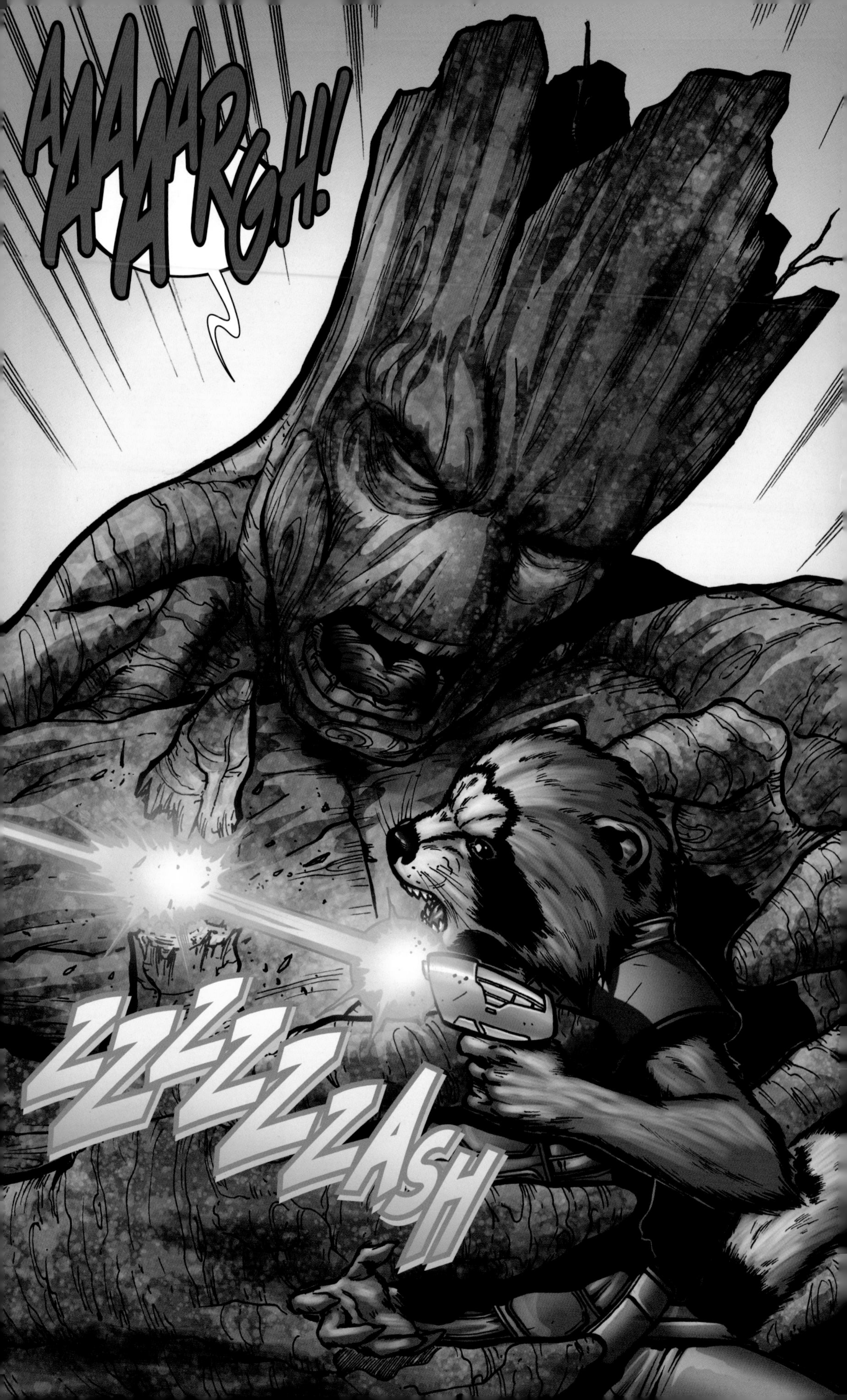
AAAARGH!
ZZZZZZASH

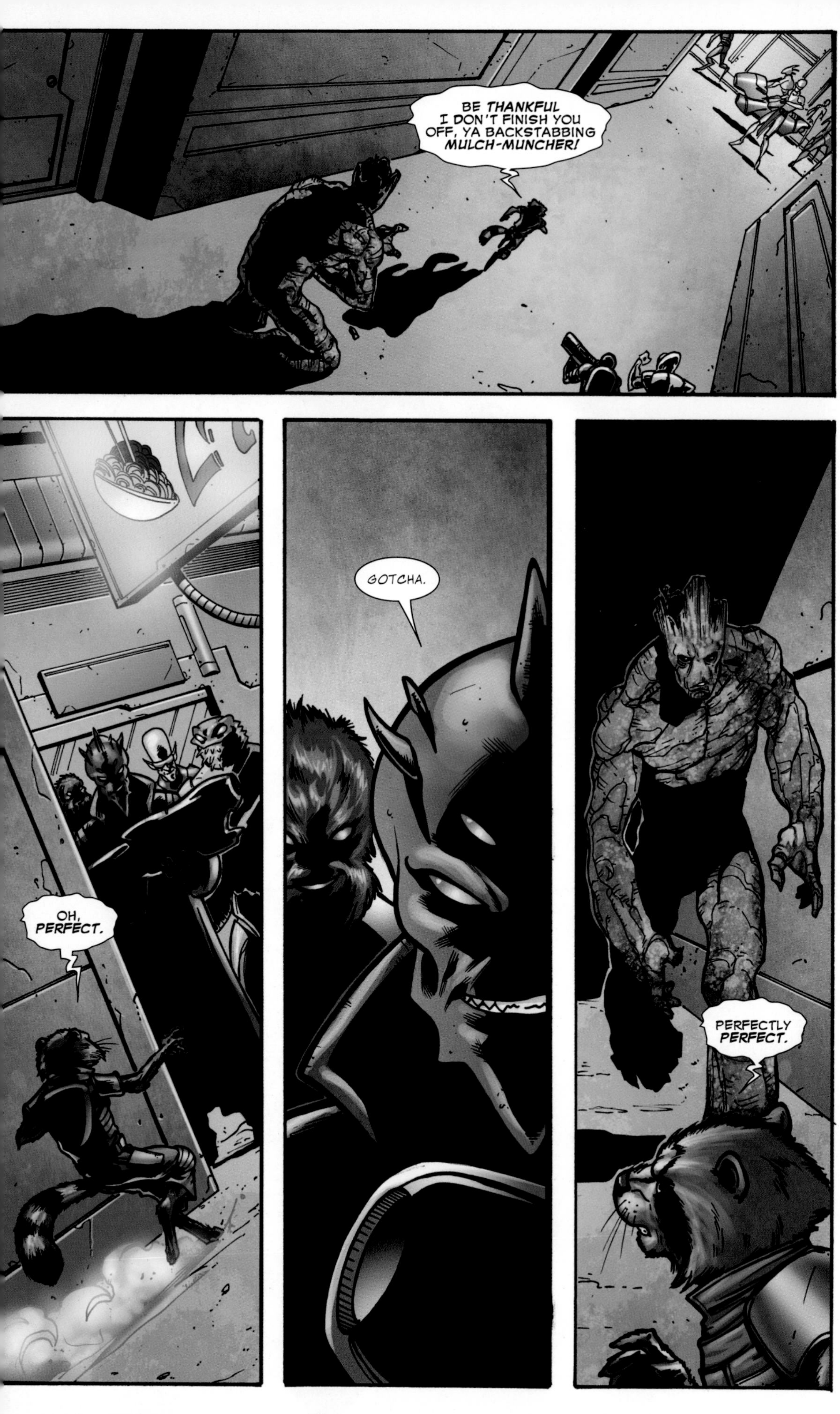
BE THANKFUL I DON'T FINISH YOU OFF, YA BACKSTABBING MULCH-MUNCHER!
OH, PERFECT.
GOTCHA.
PERFECTLY PERFECT.

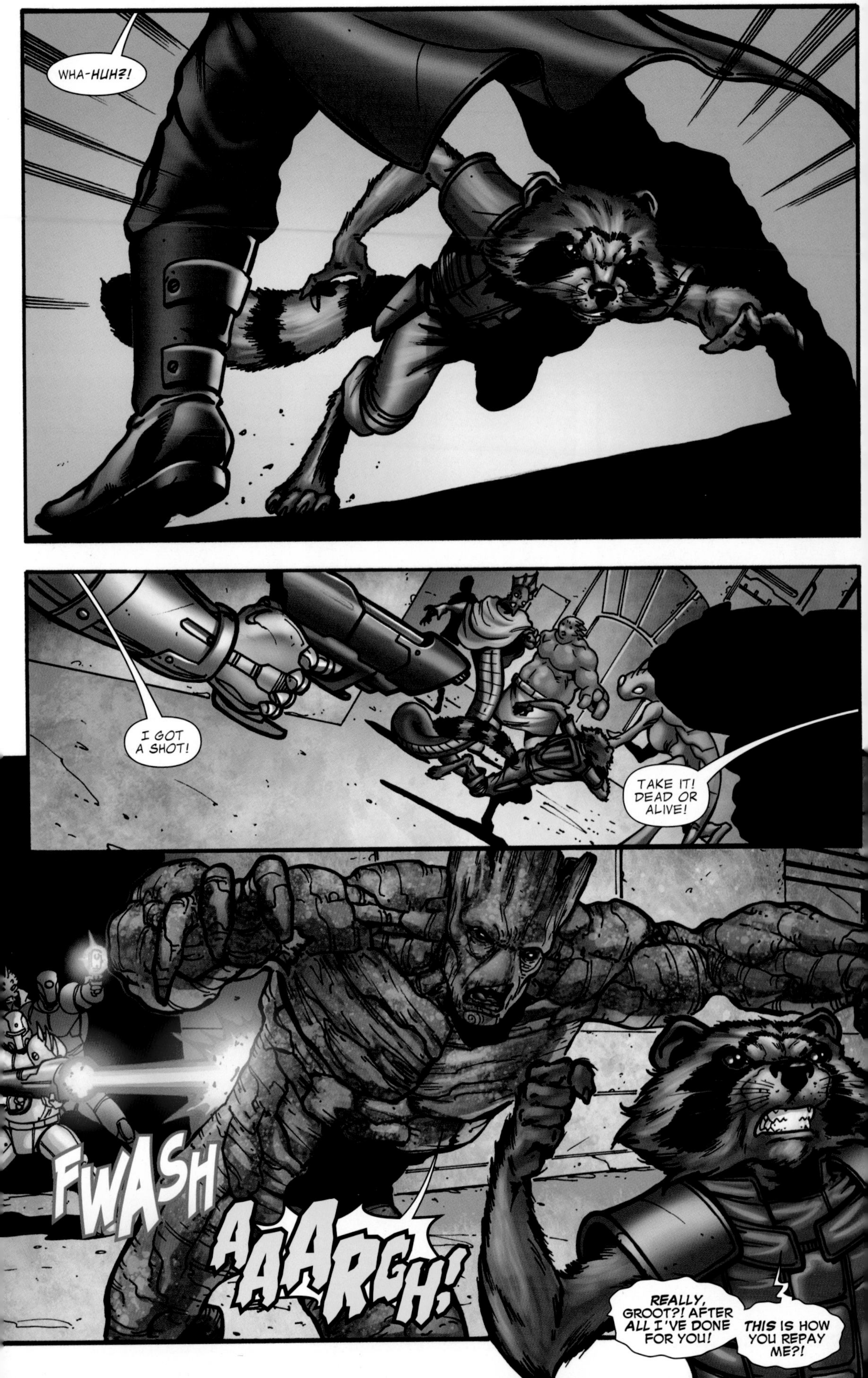

WHA-HUH?!
I GOT A SHOT!
TAKE IT! DEAD OR ALIVE!
FWASH
AAARGH!
REALLY, GROOT?! AFTER ALL I'VE DONE FOR YOU!
THIS IS HOW YOU REPAY ME?!

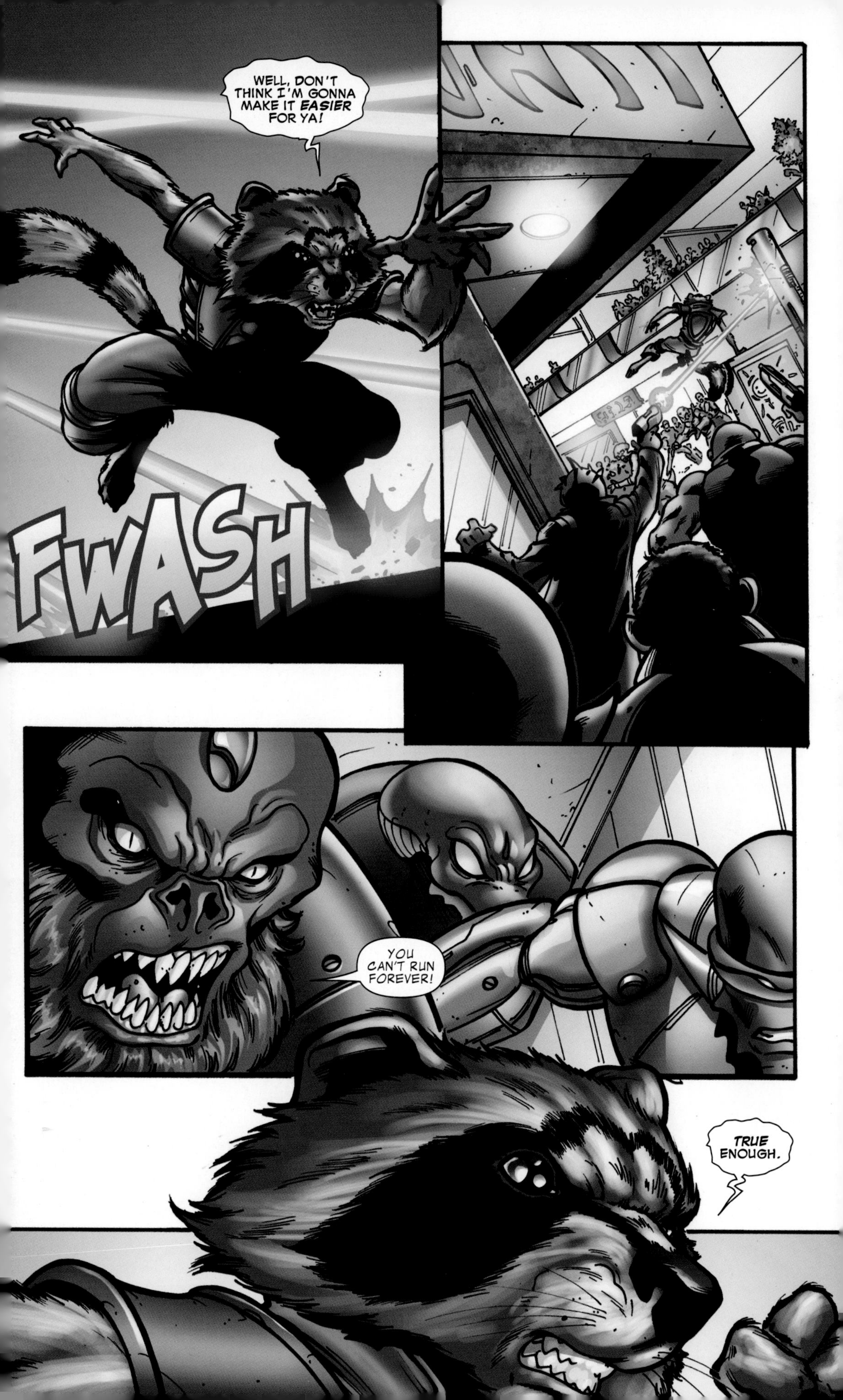
WELL, DON'T THINK I'M GONNA MAKE IT EASIER FOR YA!
FWASH
YOU CAN'T RUN FOREVER!
TRUE ENOUGH.

NOW WE'RE TALKIN'!

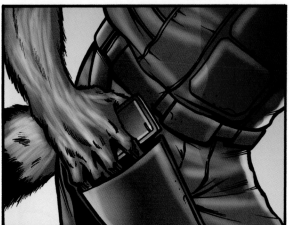

FZZT

C'MON!

HA!

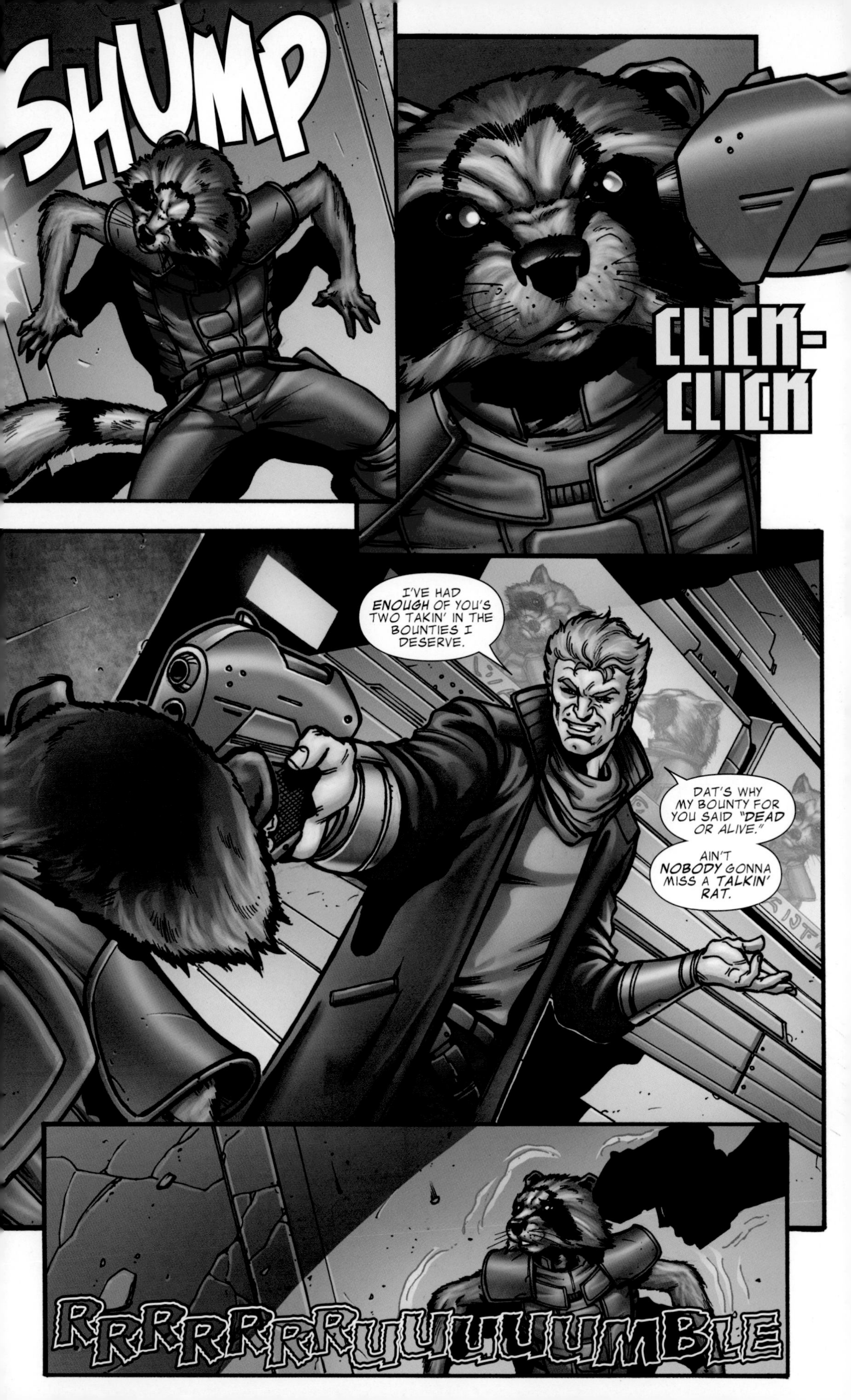
SHUMP
CLICK-CLICK
I'VE HAD ENOUGH OF YOU'S TWO TAKIN' IN THE BOUNTIES I DESERVE.
DAT'S WHY MY BOUNTY FOR YOU SAID "DEAD OR ALIVE."
AIN'T NOBODY GONNA MISS A TALKIN' RAT.
RRRRRRRRUUUUUUMBLE

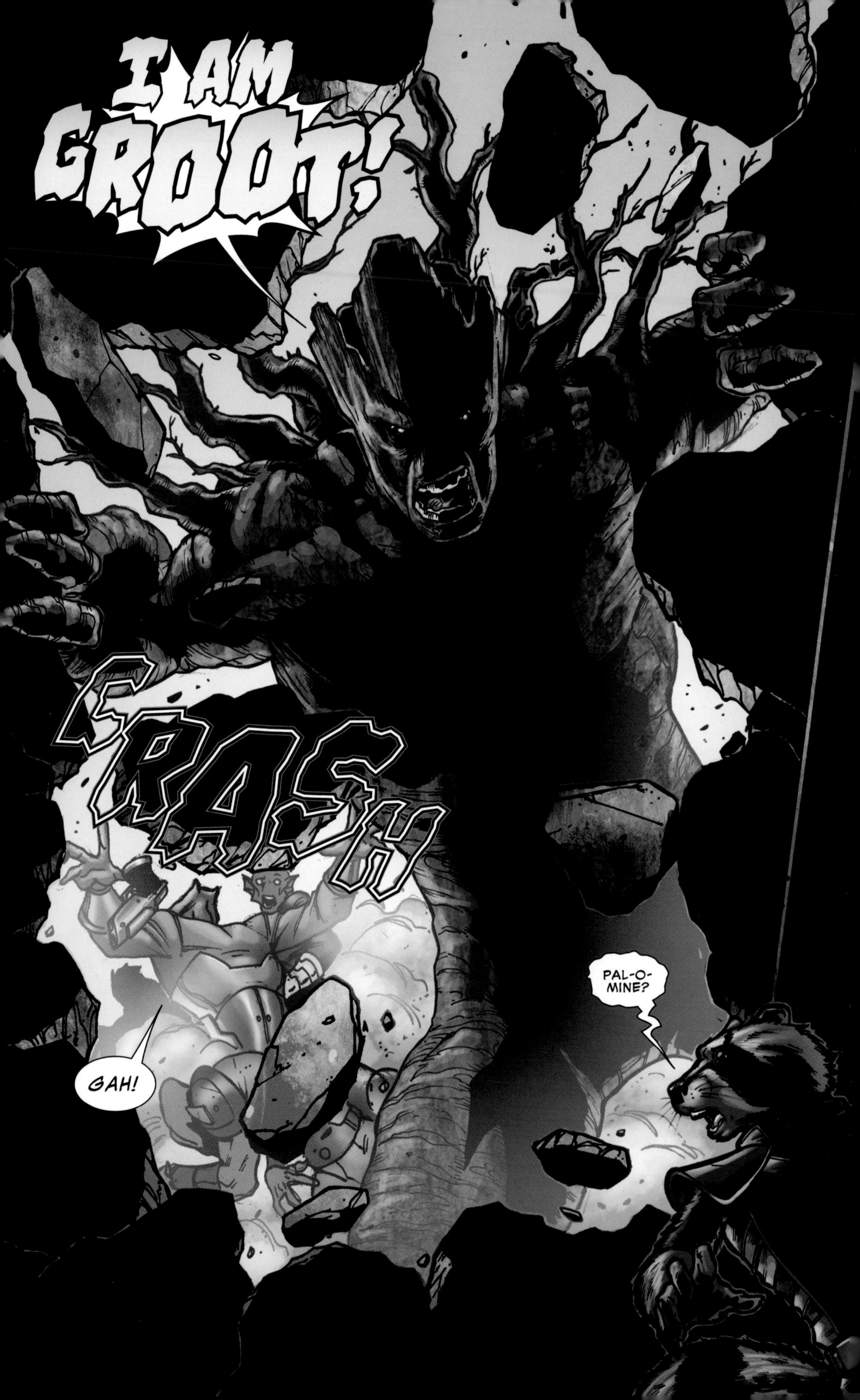
I AM GROOT!
CRASH
PAL-O-MINE?
GAH!

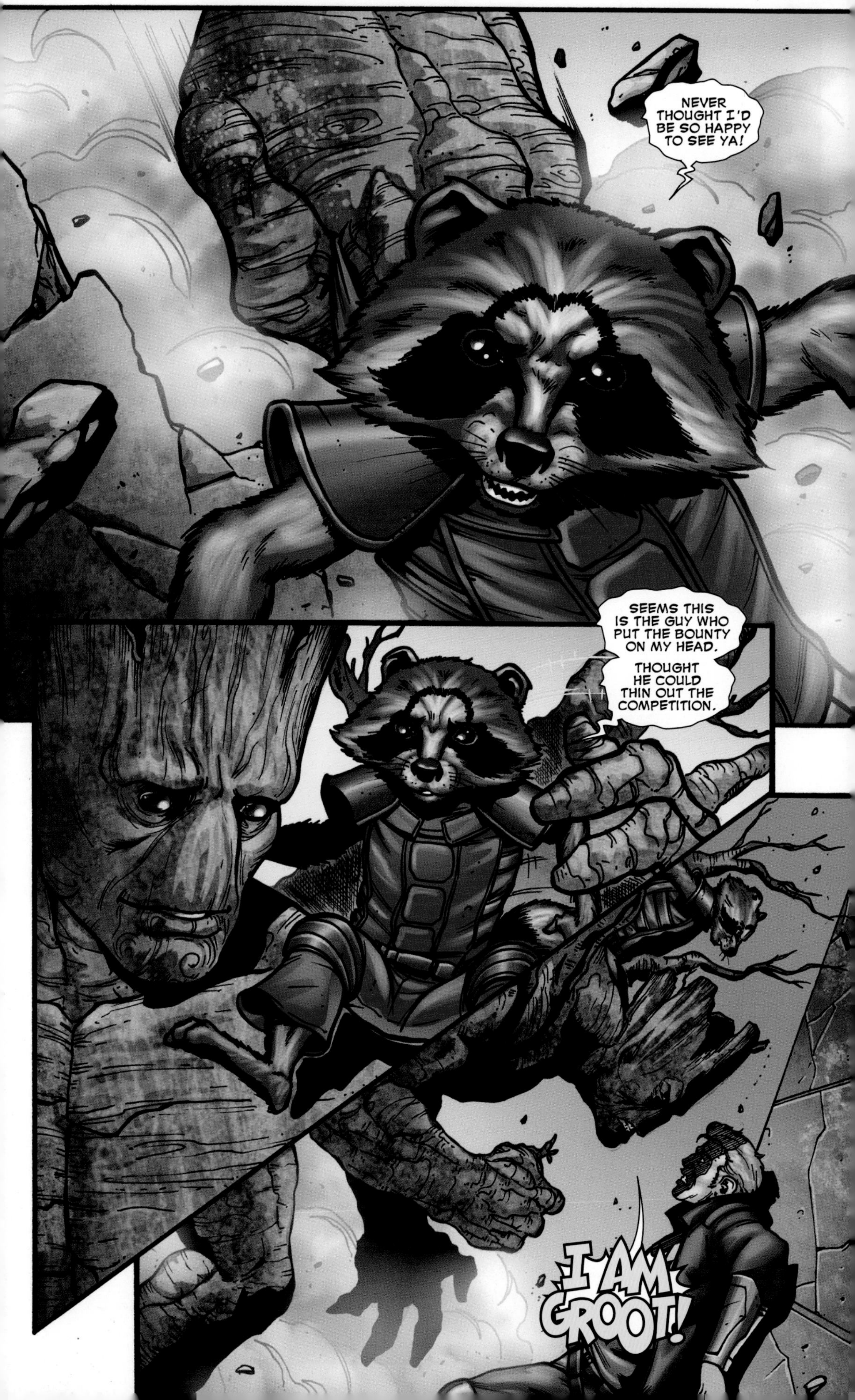
NEVER THOUGHT I'D BE SO HAPPY TO SEE YA!
SEEMS THIS IS THE GUY WHO PUT THE BOUNTY ON MY HEAD.
THOUGHT HE COULD THIN OUT THE COMPETITION.
I AM GROOT!

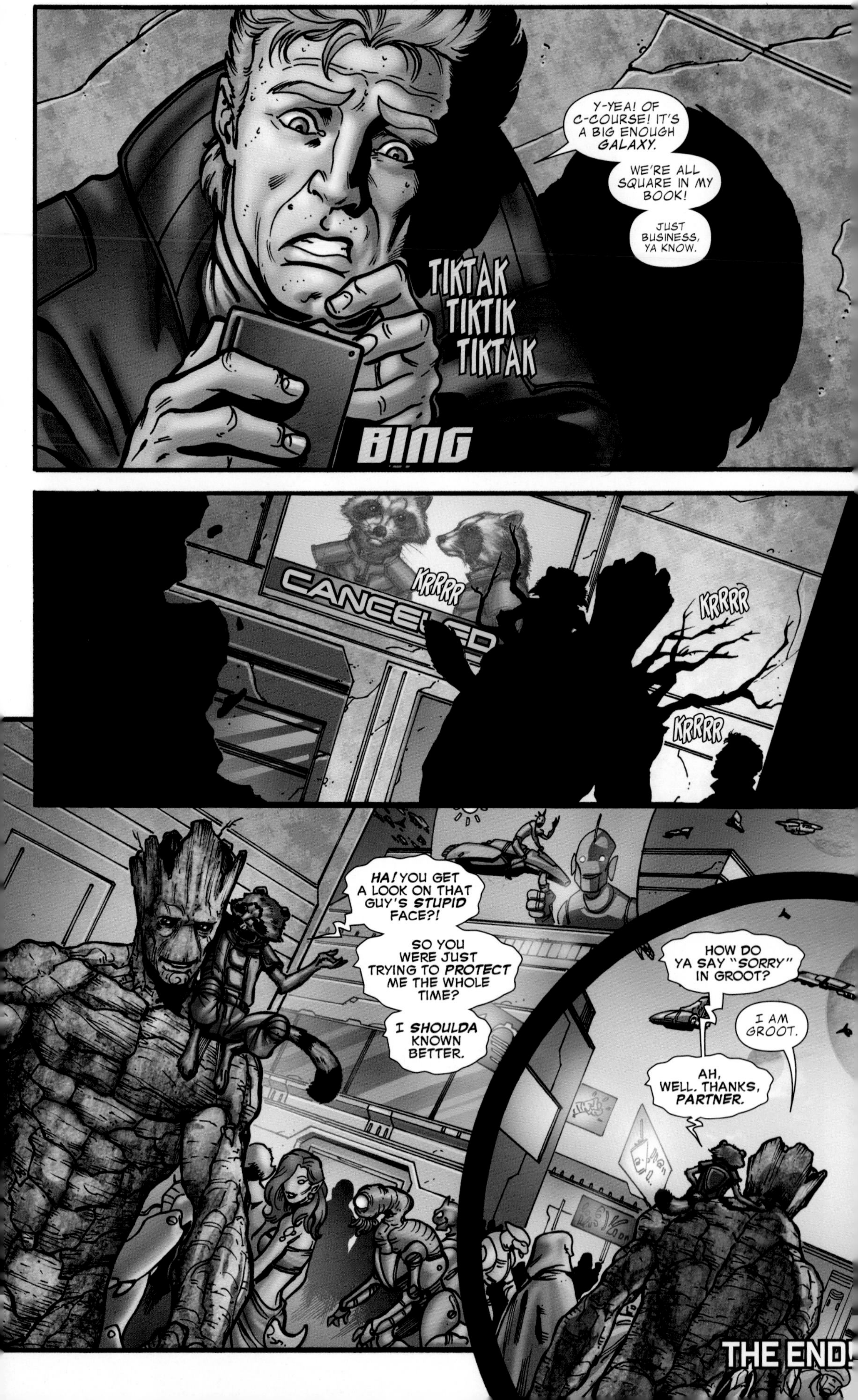
Y-YEA! OF C-COURSE! IT'S A BIG ENOUGH GALAXY.
WE'RE ALL SQUARE IN MY BOOK!
JUST BUSINESS, YA KNOW.
TIKTAK TIKTIK TIKTAK
BING
CANCELED
KRRRR
KRRRR
KRRRR
HA! YOU GET A LOOK ON THAT GUY'S STUPID FACE?!
SO YOU WERE JUST TRYING TO PROTECT ME THE WHOLE TIME?
I SHOULDA KNOWN BETTER.
HOW DO YA SAY "SORRY" IN GROOT?
I AM GROOT.
AH, WELL. THANKS, PARTNER.
THE END!

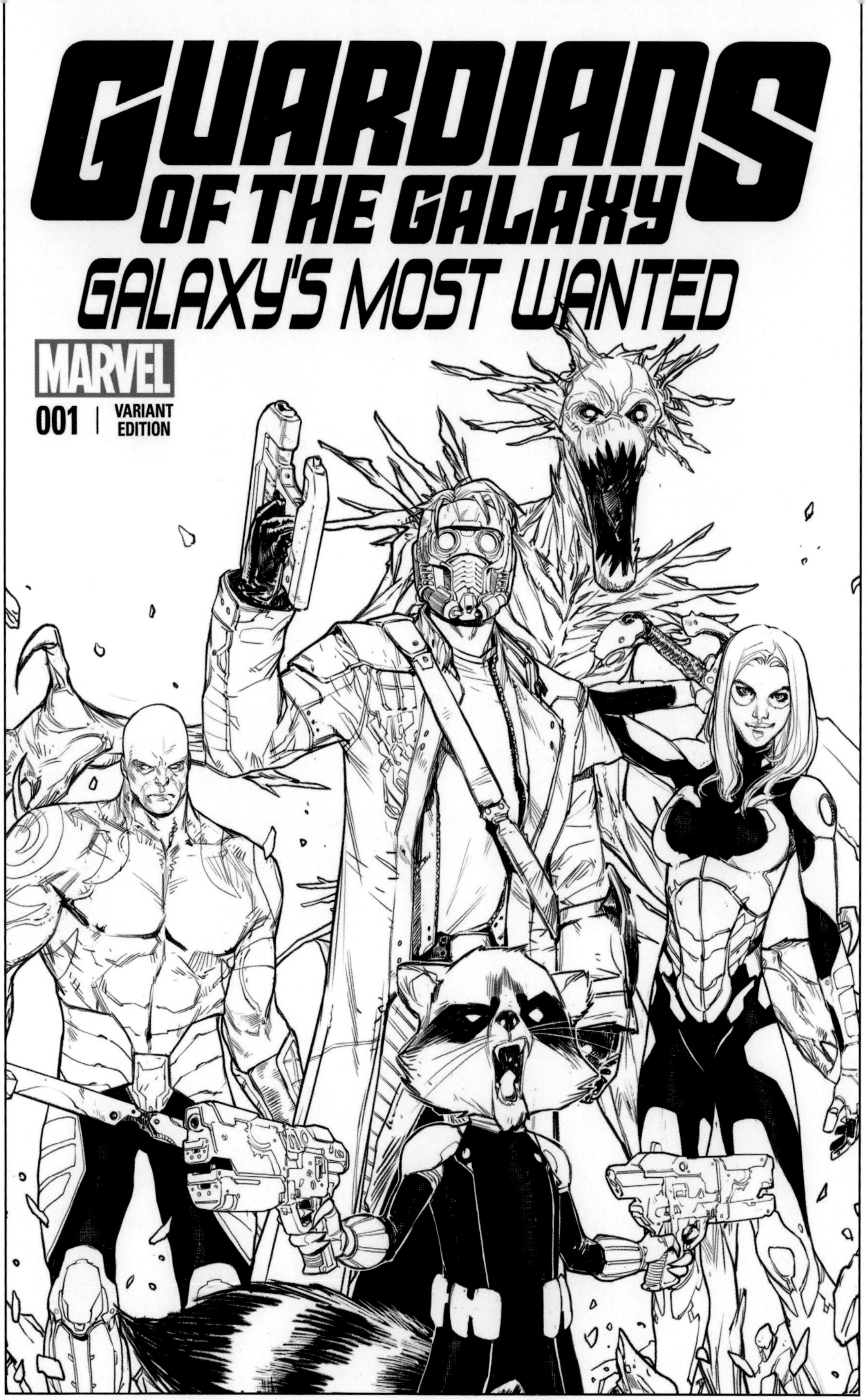
GUARDIANS
OF THE GALAXY
GALAXY'S MOST WANTED
MARVEL
001
VARIANT
EDITION

Variant Sketch Cover by Sara Pichelli

# COLLECT THEM ALL!

Hardcover Book ISBN
978-1-61479-390-8

Hardcover Book ISBN
978-1-61479-391-5

Hardcover Book ISBN
978-1-61479-392-2